The Bigfoot Mystery

To: Marvel

Enjoy the Mystery!

Best Wishes

Wayne L. Brillhart

9. 23, 2017

Written and Photographed by Wayne L. Brillhart

The Bigfoot Mystery

www.TheBirdBooks.com

Published by Wan Lee Publishing
www.wanleepublishing.com

Authored by Wayne L. Brillhart
Photography by Wayne L. Brillhart
Copy Editing by Elizabeth K. Belcher
Photo Editing by Leonard P. Norman
Graphic Design and Cover Design by Karen McDiarmid
Color Consulting by Greg Dunn

Printed and bound in the USA by Thomson Shore, Dexter, Michigan

10 9 8 7 6 5 4 3 2 1

Library of Congress Control Number: 2017902150
Brillhart, Wayne

Summary: Two English Setters, Rusty and Purdy, seek the help of the backyard birds to discover who made tracks in the snow that were ten feet apart. The photographs of ten different birds in the story assist the readers in bird recognition as they pursue the solution to the mystery.
ISBN: 978-0-9858042-2-0

1. Backyard birds—Juvenile literature.
2. Dogs—Juvenile literature.
3. Bird recognition—Juvenile literature.
4. Bigfoot—Juvenile fiction.

Manufactured by Thomson-Shore, Dexter, MI, USA; RMA16CS117, April, 2017

To those
who enjoy searching
for answers –
may they find the
real truth.

Tracks aren't always what they appear to be!

Great big footprints,
the only clue,
Left everyone here wondering,
"Who?"
Then all of a sudden
across the snow . . .

. . . it was somebody
you all know!

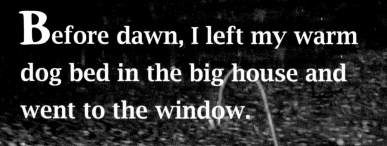

Before dawn, I left my warm dog bed in the big house and went to the window.

I looked outside and saw that the birdfeeder was on the ground covered with snow. This is not the first time the birdfeeder was down.

But this time it was broken!

And the snow was still
coming down.

Later that morning, my brother
Rusty and I went outside.

Carl the Cardinal and
Golda the Goldfinch were on the
seed platform talking about the
broken birdfeeder while
having breakfast.

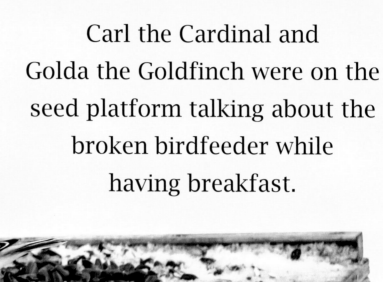

Carl saw me.

"Purdy, look at the birdfeeder.
Dottie the Doe knocked it down last time. We
need to ask her if she did it
this time."

Golda agreed.

Carl picked up another
sunflower seed.

Golda flew off and Jimmy the Junco arrived.

"Purdy, I want to know if Dottie knocked the birdfeeder down again," Jimmy tweeted. "She is big enough to do something like that. A bird couldn't knock it down."

I told Jimmy and Carl we would find out.

Roger the Red-bellied Woodpecker
arrived as Carl and Jimmy were leaving.

"We need to find Dottie and ask her
what she knows about the birdfeeder," he said.

He picked up a piece of corn and flew off to find Dottie.

We put the birdfeeder in
the basement of the
big house for repairs.

Later that morning Carl returned
to the seed platform.

"Roger found Dottie," he said.
"She will be here soon."

"Here comes Dottie,"
reported Terry
the Tufted Titmouse.

When Dottie arrived, I asked her about the birdfeeder.

"I was sleeping last night, Purdy," she said.
"I don't know who knocked it down."

I tried to think
what to do next.

We needed
some clues.

Donna the Downy Woodpecker
offered to fly to the top of a tree
to look for clues.

"Purdy," Donna called,
"I see tracks in the back of the yard.
They must be at least ten feet apart,
and they are huge!"

"They don't look
that far apart from here,"
I replied.

"You need to be up high to see,"
she answered.

Rusty decided to see for himself.
He ran to investigate.

"Donna was right," Rusty barked.
"Who could make footprints that big?"

Meanwhile, Nancy the Red-breasted Nuthatch
flew to see what Donna saw.

When Nancy came back she told everyone,
"I've seen tracks like those before
when I fly north for the summer.
I've heard they were made by Bigfoot."

Everyone became silent.

A minute later
Jimmy asked,
"Who is Bigfoot?"

Nancy flew to the repaired birdfeeder we had just put up.
Everyone listened carefully while she explained.

"Bigfoot is a huge,
hairy creature like a big ape.
He makes footprints like
the ones in the back yard.
I don't know anyone who has ever seen him.
I've never seen him."

"Oh! No! We must spread the word
that Bigfoot may be near," called Carl.

Both Jimmy and Carol the Cardinal agreed,
along with the other birds.

Terry and Charlie joined Carol and Golda
on the seed platform.

They talked about the best way to tell
their friends about Bigfoot.

Henry the Hairy Woodpecker and Charlie
were at the suet feeder talking about Bigfoot.

"You better stay high in the trees if Bigfoot is around,"
Henry told Charlie.
"That Bigfoot can reach the
lower branches of a tree, so be careful."

"Look who
just arrived!"
called Roger.

"Who are you?" I called.

"I'm Edward," the bald eagle answered.
"Word has reached me that you think Bigfoot
destroyed your birdfeeder. It wasn't Bigfoot.
He lives up north where I live."

Then Edward flew away.

We didn't know what to think.
If it wasn't Bigfoot,
then who could make tracks like that?

The birds were hungry so we
refilled the birdfeeder.

I jumped up on my doghouse
and thought
some more about
what could
have happened.

Suddenly Roger cried,
"Purdy! Look in the backyard!"

I turned to see…

… a deer we didn't know was
running away very fast into the woods.

She was gone in an instant.

Roger explained,
"The tracks that deer
made are like
the Bigfoot tracks."

"A running deer has different tracks
than a walking deer."

"So that's what happened! The deer was walking away and got scared. Then she ran fast leaving those big footprints," barked Rusty as the snow fell.

Rusty was right. When the wind blew the snow, it made the tracks look a little different so we couldn't recognize them.

With the help of our bird friends,
we solved the Bigfoot mystery.

Now,
I can finally
take a nap!

Glossary

MALE CARDINAL

FEMALE CARDINAL

Northern Cardinal

The Northern Cardinal is a seed eater. The beak has sharp edges so it can crack open the seeds. Black-oil sunflower seeds are a favorite in addition to safflower seeds, but seeds in general along with insects, fruit and grain are enjoyed by the cardinal. The cardinals prefer eating closer to the ground or on the ground. Unlike the bright red male cardinal, the female cardinal has very different markings as seen in this photograph. The Northern Cardinal is found in the Eastern and Southern United States. The male cardinal is recognized by his bright red color and black on his face while the female is buff-brown tinged with red on crest, wings and tail. Both have a distinguished crest.

Sources: 2, 3, 4, 5, 7.

American Goldfinch

The American Goldfinch loves sunflower seed and thistle seed (nyjer) and can be found at birdfeeders and thistle socks all year around. In the spring the male is a bright yellow while the female is duller yellow beneath and olive above. In winter, they are drab unstreaked brown with blackish wings and two pale wingbars. They frequent weedy fields and floodplains where thistles and asters grow. They inhabit most of the Northern and Eastern United States and Southern Canada during the summer and move south for the winter to inhabit all of the United States except a few cold Northern states.

Sources: 3, 5.

Slate-colored Dark-eyed Junco

The Dark-eyed Junco is mostly a seed-eater. They enjoy seeds of chickweed, buckwheat, lamb's quarters, and sorrel. When the Junco visits the bird feeder it prefers millet to sunflower seed, leaving them for the cardinal, chickadee and titmouse. The junco also eats insects such as beetles, moths, butterflies, caterpillars, ants, wasps and flies. Dark-eyed juncos can be found throughout the continental United States during the winter and in Canada and Alaska in the warm summer months. They can be found year around in the Northeast states, some Western states, and Northern Michigan.

Sources: 3.

MALE RED-BELLIED WOODPECKER

FEMALE RED-BELLIED WOODPECKER

Red-bellied Woodpecker

The Red-bellied Woodpecker feeds on insects and finds them in the cracks in the bark of trees. When it finds a birdfeeder it enjoys the seeds and will push away other birds except for the Blue Jay. The Red-bellied Woodpecker can be found in most areas of the United States East of the Mississippi River. The male is identified by the red covering the entire top of his head while the female has a white section on the top of her head. The female can be found in *The Deer with the Purple Nose* book.

Sources: 3.

Tufted Titmouse

The Tufted Titmouse likes seeds, suet and insects. The bigger the seed the better as the Titmouse chooses the largest seed available when at a birdfeeder. Insects eaten include caterpillars, beetles, ants, wasps, stink bugs, and treehoppers in addition to spiders and snails. Nuts, berries, acorns and beech nuts are not too big to eat. The Tufted Titmouse has a tufted crest which it can raise or lower. The Tufted Titmouse can be found in the Eastern United States.

Sources: 3, 4, 5.

Downy Woodpecker

The Downy Woodpecker enjoys suet feeders most but also black oil sunflower seeds, millet, peanuts, and chunky peanut butter in addition to pecking away for insects. They may even take a sip from an oriole or hummingbird feeder. They are black above, white below with wings spotted white and a black and white face. They have a short chisel like beak. The male has a red patch on the back of his head which distinguishes it from the female. The Downy Woodpeckers can be found throughout the United States and Canada year-round.

Sources: 4.

Red-Breasted Nuthatch

The Red-breasted Nuthatch prefers to eat insects and similar creatures such as beetles, caterpillars, spiders, ants and earwigs. When available, they also feed on the spruce bud-worm. In the fall and winter, they eat conifer seeds, many of which they hid earlier in the year. When a feeder is available the nuthatch enjoys peanuts, sunflower seeds, and suet. The Red-breasted Nuthatch is found in Canada and some Western states year around, and in all of the continental United States during the Winter.

Sources: 3.

Black-capped Chickadee

In the winter months, seeds, berries and plant matter account for more than half of the Black-capped Chickadee diet. The other half is animal food (insects, spiders, suet, and bits of meat from frozen carcasses). During the warmer months, insects, spiders, and other animal food make up most of their diet. At the bird feeder, the black oil sunflower seeds are a favorite. The Black-capped Chickadee can be found from the Northern United States and Canada to the Southern portion of Alaska.

Sources: 3, 4, 5.

Hairy Woodpecker

The Hairy Woodpecker looks very much like the Downy Woodpecker other than its much, much larger size (see Downy Woodpecker on a previous page). The Hairy Woodpecker has a long sharp bill almost as long as its head. It has a longer and more distinct black mark on the shoulder than the Downy, and usually has completely white outer tail feathers. Hairy Woodpeckers enjoy suet, peanuts, and black oil sunflower seeds in addition to insects. Like the Downy Woodpecker, the male has a patch of red on the back of his head. They can be found throughout the United States and Canada except for some desert areas and the very Northern most part of Canada.

Sources: 4.

Bald Eagle

The Bald Eagle has a white head and tail with a dark brown body and wings. The legs and bills are bright yellow. The Bald Eagle is classified as a raptor. It is not really a 'back yard bird', but the eagle was included in the book because of Bigfoot. Bald Eagles do eat carrion but their main food is fish. The Bald Eagle is found during the summer breeding season in Northern Canada. During the winter, it is found throughout the United States except for the east coast.

Sources: 4, 7.

References/Bibliography

1. National Audubon Society Pocket Guide: Familiar Birds of North America – East Ann H. Whitman, Editor. A Borzoi Book. Published by Alfred A. Knopf, Inc. 1986. Eleventh Printing 2000.

2. An Audubon Handbook Eastern Birds John Farrand, Jr. A Chanticleer Press Edition. McGraw-Hill Book Company 1988.

3. The Cornell Lab of Ornithology website All About Birds. http://www.allaboutbirds.org

4. Bird Source. Birding with a Purpose web site. www.birdsource.org . http://www.birdsource.org/gbbc/learning/bird-feeding-tips/what-kind-of-birdfood-should-i-use

5. A Field Guide to the Birds of Eastern and Central North America. 5th Edition. Roger Tory Peterson and Virginia Marie Peterson. Houghton Mifflin. 1980, 2002.

6. National Bird-Feeding Society website: http://www.birdfeeding.org/nbfm/most-wanted-americas-top-ten-backyard-birds/attracting-americas-top-ten-backyard-birds/house-finch.html

7. National Audubon Society Field Guide to North American Birds: Western Region Ann H. Whitman, Editor. A Chanticleer Press Edition. Published by Alfred A. Knopf, Inc. 1977. Second Edition.

For information on Sasquatch (Bigfoot North America) and Yeti (Bigfoot of Asia, also called 'The Abominable Snowman") visit www.TheBirdBooks.com/Bigfoot. If you use the information be sure to quote the source.

Acknowledgements

Thanks first of all to my accommodating wife Patricia who put up with having the window up and the screen off in the bathroom almost 'every time she turned around'. After all, it was winter and quite cold! The author was able to get great shots through the window being reasonably well hidden (with his heavy coat on). Also thanks for her valuable input on the story.

Thanks to Leonard P. Norman for assisting with preliminary photo preparation. Thanks to Elizabeth Belcher for her great editing skills. Thanks to Karen McDiarmid for her great work on the graphic design and cover; and thanks to Greg Dunn (http://www.digimagery.com) for his assistance with color management and preparation for the printer. A big thanks to my cousin Larry Houseman who took me to a spot to get the eagle photos. Also thanks to all of our previous customers who have waited so long for *The Bigfoot Mystery.*

Where the Book Came From

It was another cold winter day and another 12 inches of snow had fallen on top of the existing snow. The bird feeder was down, so I went out side with my camera to take some shots and discovered that the birdfeeder needed some repairs. There were lots of tracks in the snow making it difficult to tell what happened. I took the birdfeeder to the basement workshop to fix it.

It was later that I was in the backyard looking beyond Purdy's doghouse in the wide, open spaces that I noticed some large tracks in the snow. At first I thought of two of my grandsons who wear size 14 shoes; but these footprints were nearly twice that size! Also, they were over ten feet apart! The snow around the footprints was untouched so the prints had to be real—not made by someone just for fun.

For three weeks, I pondered the question, "Who made those huge footprints?" I finally resolved the answer with this clue. The footprints were not staggered like a person (or animal) walking. The prints were one directly ahead of another. By now I had decided this was the new mystery story: "The Bigfoot Mystery". I proceeded to take lots of photos of Rusty and Purdy and the birds to come up with the rest of the story. Read the end of the story for the final explanation of what happened.

Rusty & Purdy Backyard Bird Adventures
by Wayne L. Brillhart

The Mystery at the Birdfeeder
The Deer with the Purple Nose
The Bigfoot Mystery

www.TheBirdBooks.com

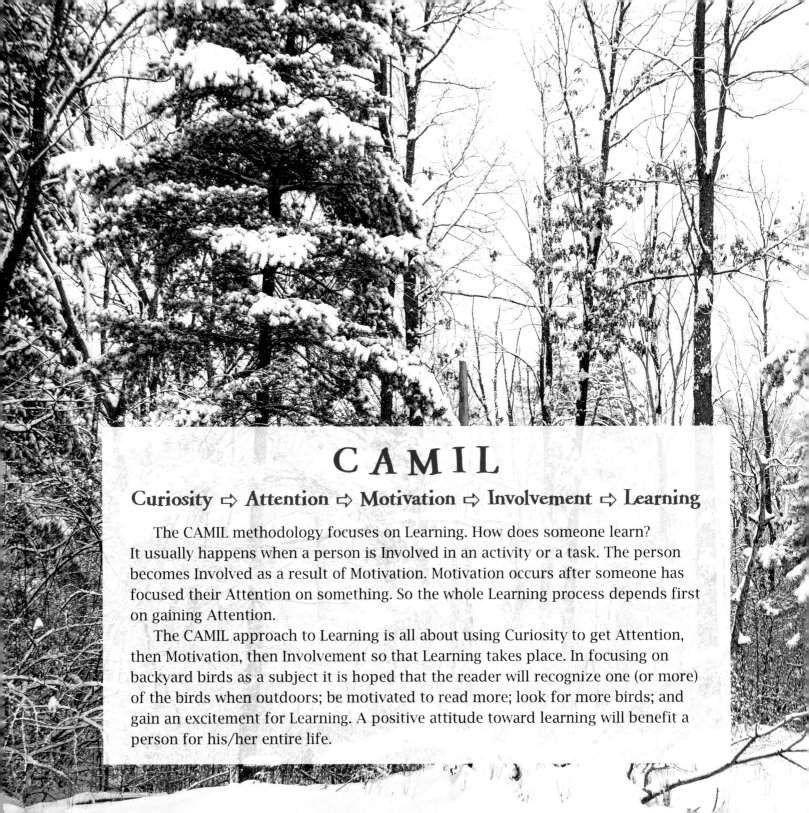

CAMIL

Curiosity ⇨ **Attention** ⇨ **Motivation** ⇨ **Involvement** ⇨ **Learning**

The CAMIL methodology focuses on Learning. How does someone learn? It usually happens when a person is Involved in an activity or a task. The person becomes Involved as a result of Motivation. Motivation occurs after someone has focused their Attention on something. So the whole Learning process depends first on gaining Attention.

The CAMIL approach to Learning is all about using Curiosity to get Attention, then Motivation, then Involvement so that Learning takes place. In focusing on backyard birds as a subject it is hoped that the reader will recognize one (or more) of the birds when outdoors; be motivated to read more; look for more birds; and gain an excitement for Learning. A positive attitude toward learning will benefit a person for his/her entire life.